To:

From:

I Love You, My Little
UNICORN

words by
Rose Rossner

pictures by
Morgan Huff

sourcebooks
wonderland

My precious little unicorn,

you make the world so bright.

You dazzle in the sparkling sky,

spreading joy with all your light.

I wished upon a **lucky star**,

for a special one like you.

With lots of giggles and glitter,

I love you through and through.

I hope that you'll remember,

as you blossom, bloom, and grow,

life's important little things,

that I want you to know…

I **believe** in all you do,

and who you want to be.

I'll be here to cheer you on.

Stay young and wild and free!

With you I'd travel near and far,

and take each day in stride.

You're my greatest adventure,

I'll be forever by your side.

I hope you know you are **enough**.

Beautiful, **strong**, and **wise**.

And even though times can get tough,

I know you'll always rise.

Use your **voice**, so loud and proud.

Let out your biggest neigh!

Be the leader of the pack.

You show US the way.

My darling little unicorn,

I am so **proud** of you.

Always try your very best,

there's nothing you can't do.

Some days are warm and sunny,

and others wet and gray.

No matter what we face together,

with you I'll always stay.

It's okay to get messy,

and make a million mistakes.

You'll learn from them and grow so much.

Choose the path you want to take.

Don't forget to ask for help,

if the load's too much to bear.

You are never ever by yourself,

there's work that we can **share**.

If you need me just to listen,

I'll sit quietly with you.

No matter what, I'll be here.

My love for you is true.

My happy, lucky unicorn,

you are the greatest friend.

Share with others, be kind, have fun...

Wish the days would never end.

Never dull your sparkle.

Let your inner rainbow shine!

Remember—always be yourself,

sweet unicorn of mine.

I Love You, My Little Unicorn.

You are my shooting star.

Full of twinkle magic,

I love you for who you are!

For my Sadie Rose, may all of your unicorn dreams come true. XO —RR

To Mom, for always helping my sparkle shine bright. —MH

Published by Sourcebooks Wonderland, an imprint of Sourcebooks Kids
P.O. Box 4410, Naperville, Illinois 60567–4410
(630) 961-3900
sourcebookskids.com

Cataloging-in-Publication Data is on file with the Library of Congress.

Source of Production: Wing King Tong Paper Products Co. Ltd., Shenzhen, Guangdong Province, China
Date of Production: November 2021
Run Number: 5023490

Printed and bound in China.
WKT 10 9 8 7 6 5 4 3 2 1